Naughty Spot! It's dinner time. Where can he be?

Is he behind the door?

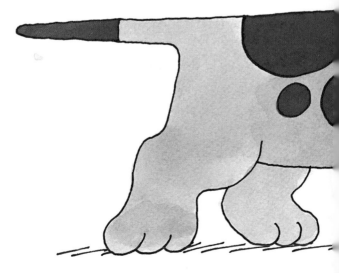

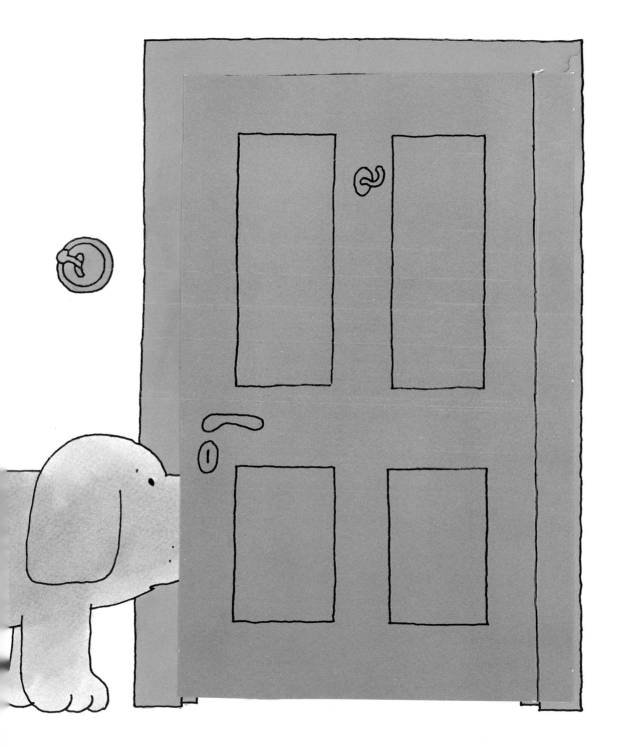

Is he inside the clock?

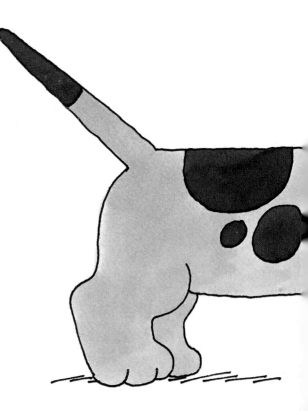

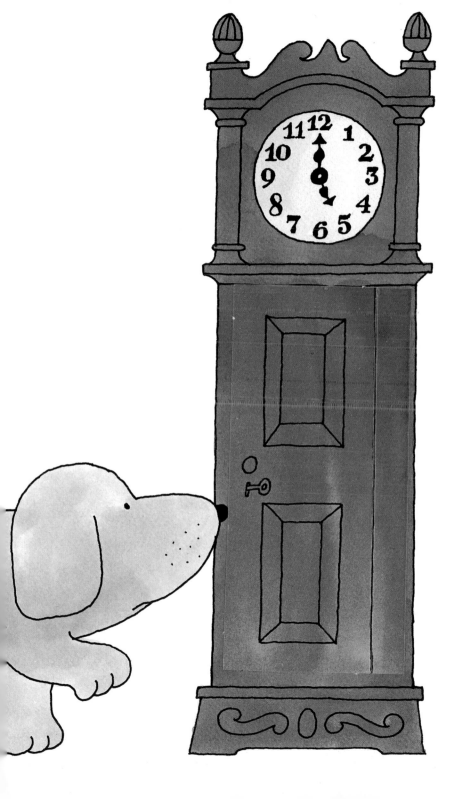
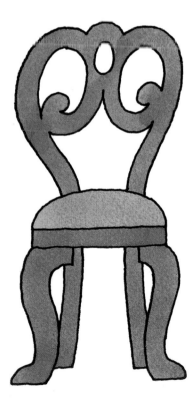

Is he in the piano?

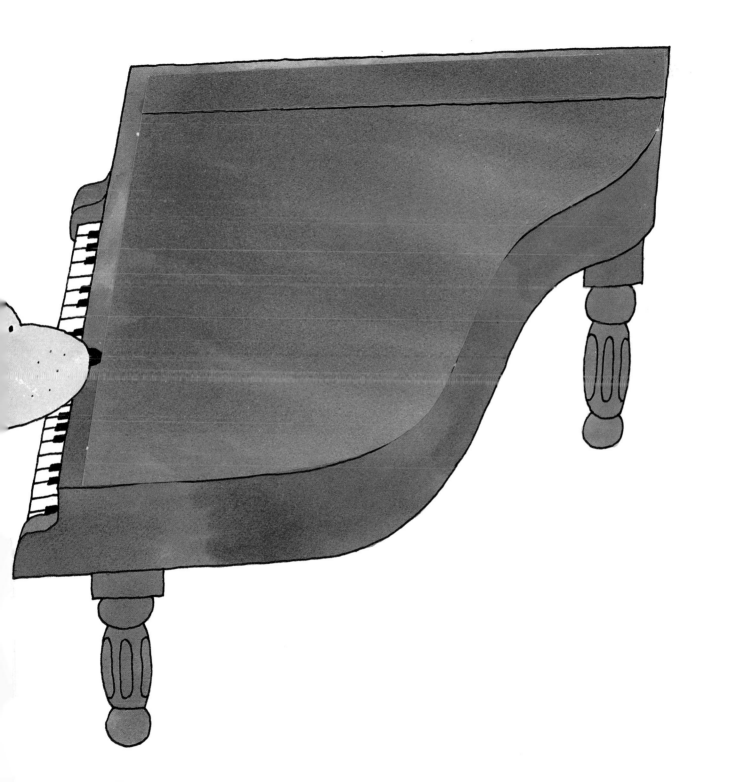

Is he under the stairs?

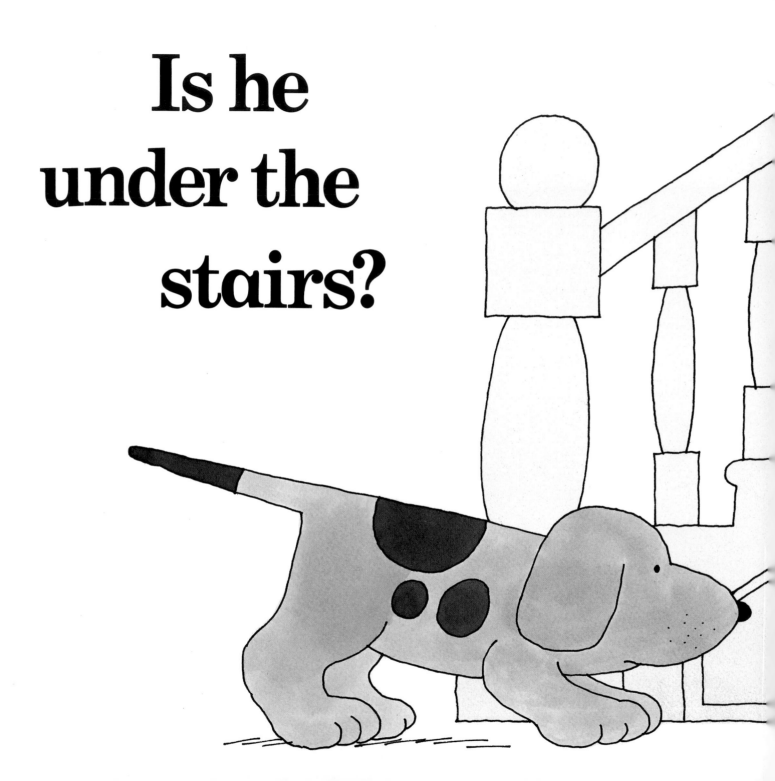

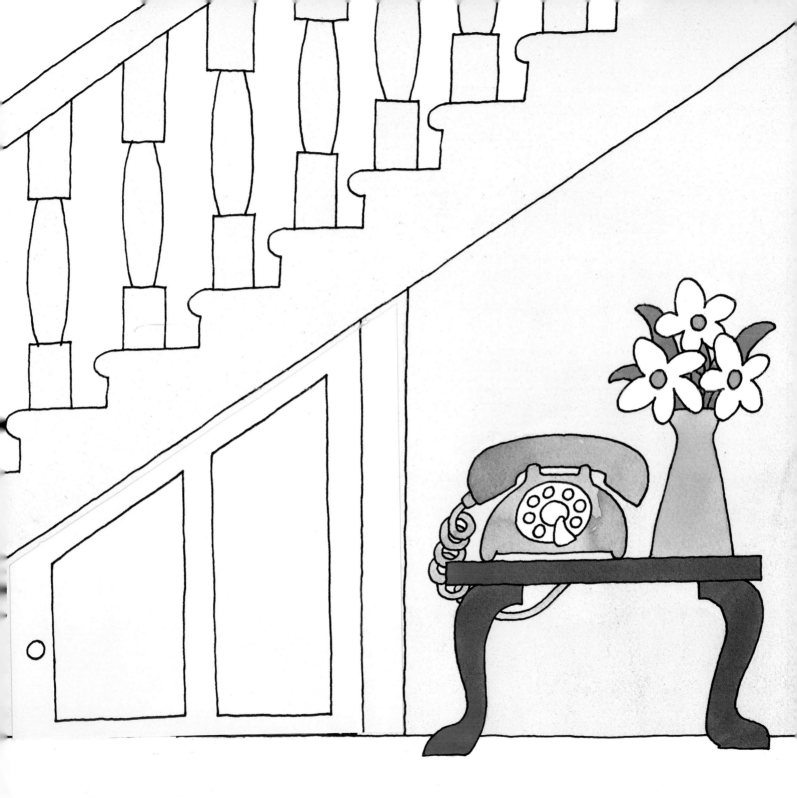

Is he
in the wardrobe?

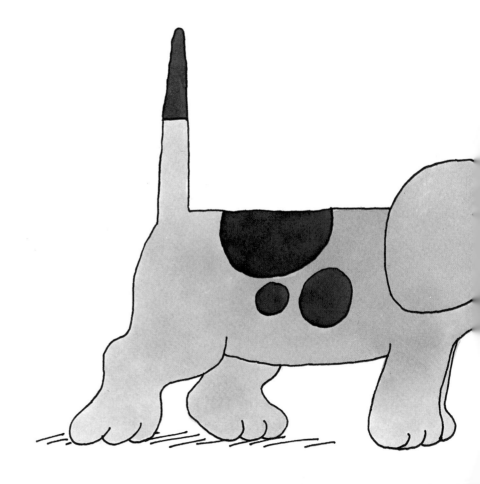

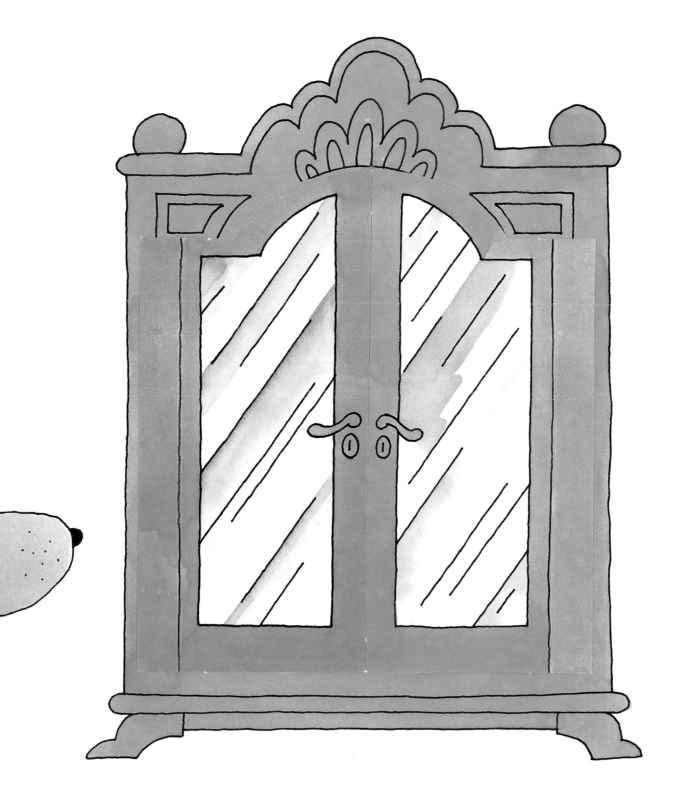

Is he under the bed?

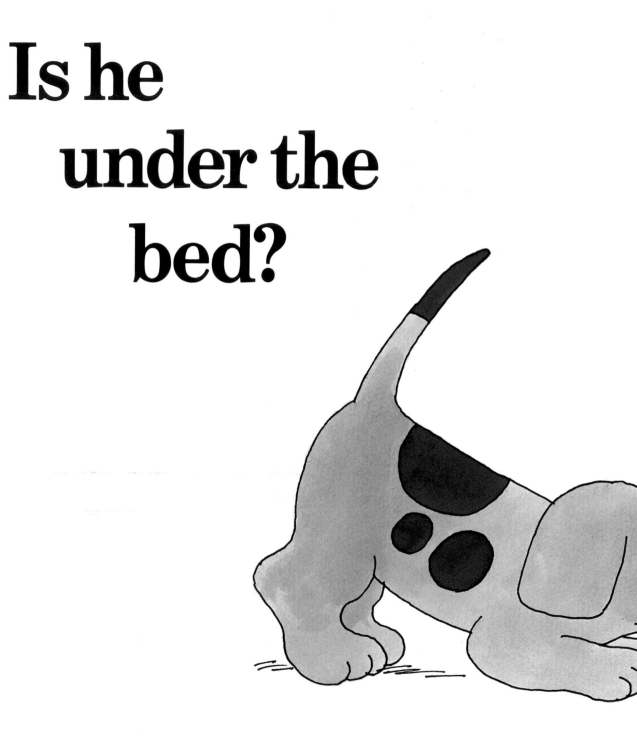

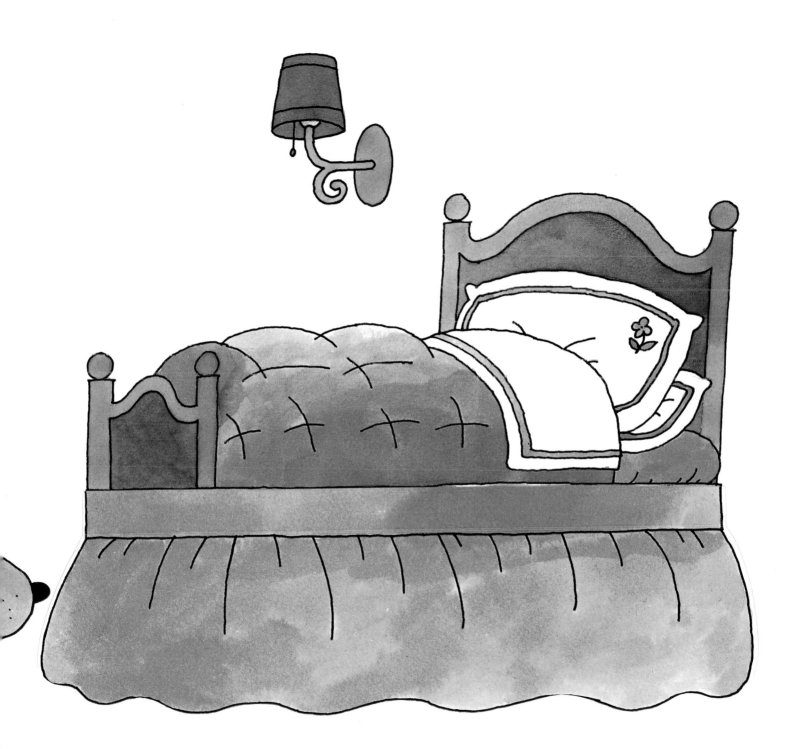

Is he in the box?

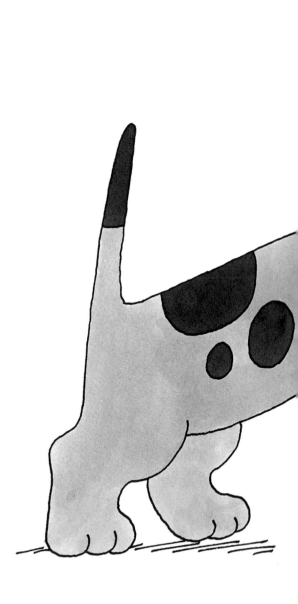

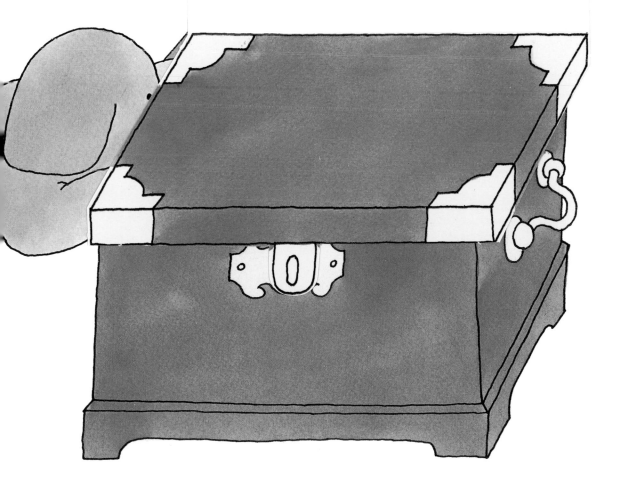

There's Spot!

He's under the rug.

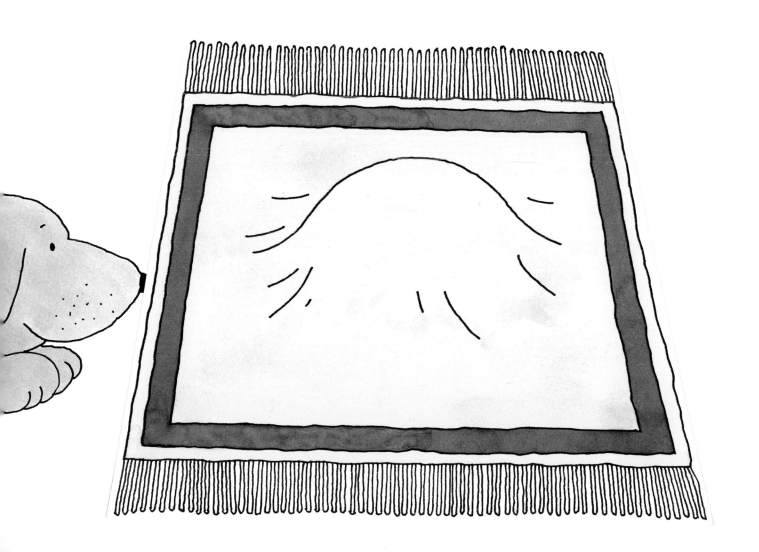

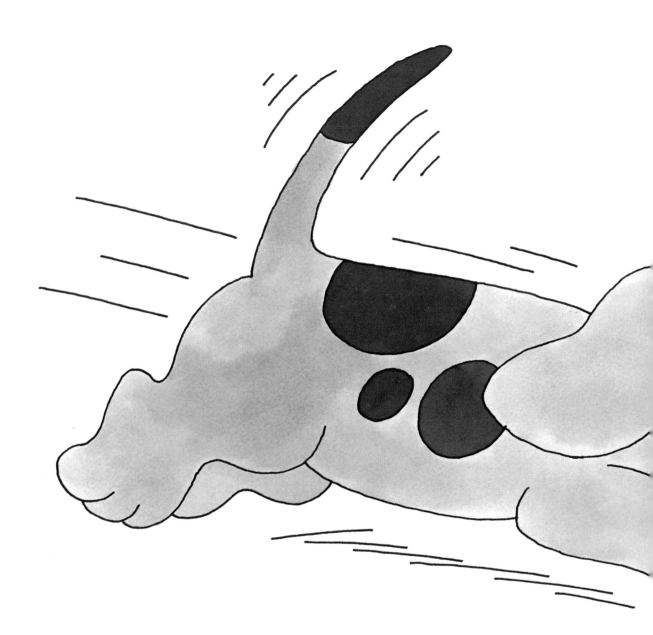

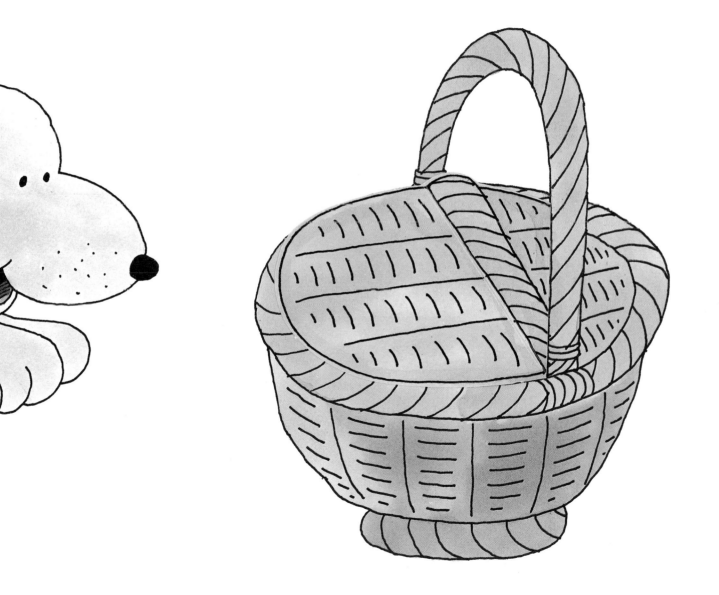

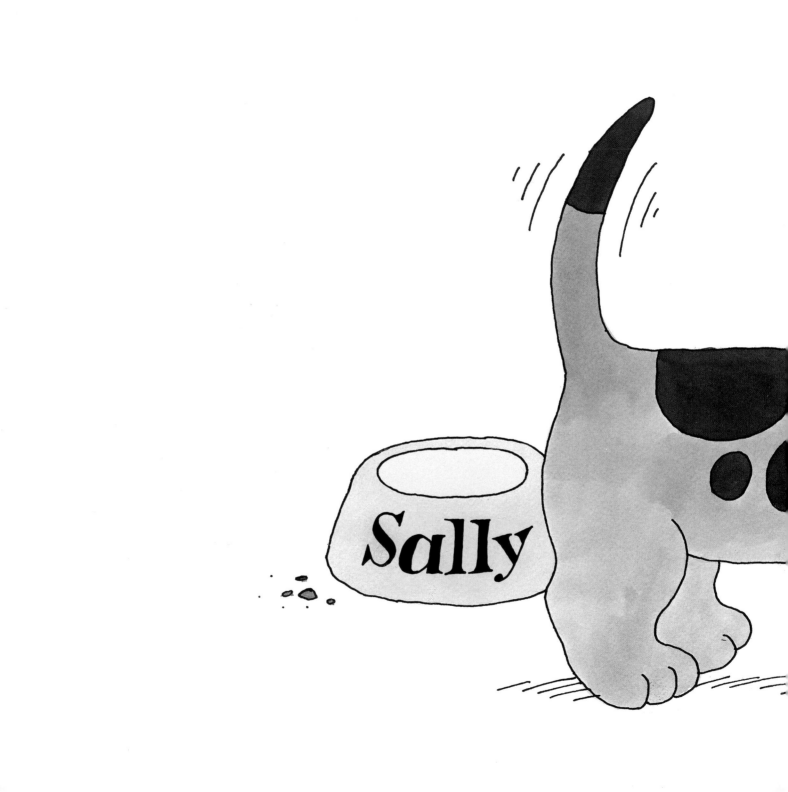